TALES OF THE WITCH'S CAT

THE PUPPY PROBLEM

Kirstie Watson   Tilia Rand-Bell

TELLTALE TOTS

Telltale Tots Ltd.
www.telltaletots.co.uk

First published in the United Kingdom by Telltale Tots
Publishing 2022

ISBN: 978-1-914937-11-8

A CIP catalogue record for this book is available from the
British Library.

Cover design by Ryan Webb:
www.corrynwebbillustration.co.uk

To Loxie,

My little fluffy writing buddy and the
inspiration for Puppy.

And to everyone who loves their
furry friends – mischief and all!

Kirstie

I love The Witch's Cat because...

The magic always goes wrong and it makes me laugh.

Alex, age 6

A fun and curious cat that keeps on giving.

Ellamay King, age 7

He is naughty.

Jackson Moore, age 7

I like it that the cat tries to make soup but it goes wrong! It's funny he turns into different animals!

Veya, age 7

He is cheeky and funny!

Jessica Smith, age 9

I love the spells.

Lola, age 7

He's not very good at magic and he always makes a mess.

Ben Peterson, age 8

When I look at the front cover it inspires me to become a witch.

Aaliyah Cooke, age 6

Meet the characters of the story!

The Witch's Cat

The Lovely Witch

Puppy

The Wizard of The Woods

Orion

The Stern Librarian

Chapter 1

It's Me,
The Witch's Cat

Hello, it's me, The Witch's Cat. Some people also call me Cat, or sometimes CAAAAT, if they're really unhappy with me – which, thankfully, isn't very often.

Well, actually, I did get into a teeny bit of trouble only yesterday. I thought I'd surprise The Lovely Witch with a nice cup of 'special tea'.

1

I love doing nice things for her. When I say, 'special tea', what I really mean is just putting a load of things that looked and smelled interesting into a teapot, then adding hot water. I added some hairy, dried mushrooms, old toenail clippings, a ball of dust and some other things I can't remember. When I handed her the cup, she was really happy about it at first, but after the first sip, she started trotting around the house and whinnying like a horse. That did end in a CAAAAT – once the tea had worn off.

And then there was the time that I decided to make The Lovely Witch some lunch. That didn't quite go to plan either. If there is one thing I've learned it's

ALWAYS make sure that you're looking at a cookbook and NOT a spellbook. It's an easy mistake to make, and using the wrong book can lead to a cooking CATASTROPHE. trust me. After that, The Lovely Witch said, 'CAT, you are NEVER allowed to make lunch EVER again!' I don't think she really meant it – do you?

Then there was the time I made a broomstick blunder. The Lovely Witch makes broomstick flying look really easy and so much FUN – so I couldn't help but try it myself.

As you might guess, that didn't work out too well either. I ended up taking a terrifying trip around the world, clinging onto the broomstick for my life. Afterwards, The Lovely Witch said, 'Cats are not supposed to ride broomsticks on their own!' I do agree with her on that.

Ah, yes, there was also that time I found an old wand in a drawer; one slip and I accidentally sent myself back to the time of the dinosaurs. I could say more, but that's a story for another day.

As you get to know me, you'll find that I'm a good, thoughtful cat who ALWAYS tries his best. The problem is that even when I try my best, things don't usually go to plan. Well, to tell you the truth, I don't do plans. Once I've got an idea, I just dive in without too much thinking. What did The Lovely Witch say yesterday after the 'special tea' thing? Ah yes: 'Oh, Cat, you do try, but I WISH you would think things through and ask me before meddling with magic.' I probably should, shouldn't I? It might save me from getting into so much trouble.

Where was I? Ah yes, I was talking about ME. I'm a sleek, ginger cat and I like to do things all cats usually do: eat and sleep during the day (in my favourite sunny spot) and go on adventures during the night. The Lovely Witch is in charge around here, but she's always very busy with the things that witches usually do. So that leaves me plenty of time for my night-time adventures.

Yes, sometimes this does involve playing with **MAGIC**. And because I'm not really allowed to, it makes it even **MORE** exciting. And it may come as a surprise, but I don't find magic very easy. Which is why I like to practise whenever I can – I'm not one to give up just because something is difficult. I'll always try my best – even if it means making a few mistakes along the way. I prefer to think of it as 'learning as I go'. Unfortunately, The Lovely Witch disagrees. Before she leaves me alone, she usually says, 'Absolutely **DO NOT** do any magic of any sort for any reason whatsoever! Magic is totally and utterly **BANNED.'**

It might sound like The Lovely Witch is always grumpy, but that's not true. She is really, **REALLY** lovely – not mean or wicked like some witches. She's kind and gives the best ear scratches. She's patient too, and is always there to help me fix any little magical mishaps.

The Lovely Witch and I live in a cottage by the woods, not far from a magical little town. I rarely go to town on my own, though; I prefer to stay close

to home and travel no further than my favourite sunny spot in the garden. The only time I go anywhere else is with The Lovely Witch. I especially like to keep her company at her Annual Witching Meeting. It's my favourite trip of the year. There is always lots of magic and mischief to be had, and I can't WAIT for the next one.

For as long as I can remember, it's

been just the two of us – The Lovely Witch and me. We live together in perfect harmony. The Lovely Witch cares for me, and in return, I help make her life more interesting. She'd never admit it, but I think her life would be totally boring without me. We make a great team – a witch and a cat, which is just how it is supposed to be.

But that's enough of all that. Now you know a bit about me, it's time I fill you in on my latest misadventure.

It started yesterday… maybe, or was it last week? I'm not sure. Being a cat, I don't follow regular time, you see. I don't know about minutes, hours, days, weeks or months. It doesn't mean anything to me. That's because some minutes take

FOREVER, don't they!? Like when The Lovely Witch says, 'Dinner will be ready in just a minute!' That minute might as well be five hours. Or sometimes, when you are not looking forward to something, the time goes by far too quickly. Like when you're waiting for the effects of some 'special tea' to wear off because you know you're going to be in trouble. Time makes no sense to me.

Anyway, back to what happened. It began just after my tuna breakfast. The Lovely Witch arrived home with what she said was 'a wonderful surprise!' She was carrying a large cardboard box that had a worrying smell. It also seemed to be making some snuffling and squeaky yapping noises. Weird.

'Look what I've got!' The Lovely Witch said as she began to lift off the lid. I already knew that something was very wrong, but then she said the words no cat EVER wants to hear...

Chapter 2

The Arrival

'Cat, I want you to meet our new... PUPPY!' said The Lovely Witch.

A... puppy? I couldn't believe what I was hearing. I peered inside the box and was met by a disgusting, slobbery lick across my face. Yuck.

'Ahh, she likes you!' The Lovely Witch said – like that was a good thing. 'Go on, why don't you lick her back?'

Does she know me AT ALL? I wondered. I don't like puppies, and there was NO WAY I was going to lick one.

Just then, the puppy leaped out from the box and started jumping all over me like some kind of wild beast. It was awful.

The puppy was the size of a small cuddly toy, with big brown eyes and floppy ears. It was like a big ball of fluff, but with tiny little paws and a curled-up tail. Some might say it was 'cute', but I

don't like puppies, so I definitely would **NOT** say that.

'I think we'll call her... Puppy,' said The Lovely Witch, whilst giving the little beast one of **MY** favourite ear scratches.

'That's not a very good name,' I huffed under my breath.

The puppy soon tired of leaping about and settled down for a nap... in **MY** favourite sunny spot! I couldn't believe it! I should have warned it that it was **MY** spot, but I didn't want to wake it up. So, instead, I sneaked off to a quiet place in the garden.

A little while later . . .

As I lay there, trying to have a lovely whatever-time-of-day-it-is snooze (as I like to call it), a bad thought crept into my head. Was I being replaced by the puppy? Surely not. We were family, weren't we? The Lovely Witch and I – just the two of us – happy together. But perhaps The Lovely Witch was looking for a more playful pet – she seemed to love how Puppy played. And she couldn't keep both of us, could she? After all, witches usually only have ONE pet – hardly ever two. Perhaps the 'special tea' had been the last straw, and now she planned to get rid of me. I felt so sad and confused.

Just then, I noticed a small shadow was blocking out the sun. I looked up to see the puppy standing over me. Her tongue was hanging out, and she had a worrying look in her eye.

'Ahhh, she wants to play with you, Cat!' said The Lovely Witch from the doorway. 'Go on, why don't you have some fun and play together for a while?'

WHAT? When was the last time she saw me... play!?

Then, without warning, Puppy jumped on top of me. It was quite a shock. 'Got woo!' she said, giggling. 'Bet woo can't get me!' she teased.

'So, it talks too! Great,' I huffed. 'NO, I probably can't "get woo" because I don't want to. Cats do NOT play with puppies. And I was just having a lovely whatever-time-of-day-it-is snooze, so GO AWAY!'

But Puppy wasn't listening to a word I said. She just pounced on me again and again! I was about to tell her off, but then she surprised me with a playful nip to the tail. Then she ran away sniggering, 'Got woo!'

'You come back here and say sorry… that was NOT very kind!' I shouted, following her into the bushes.

But going after her was a big mistake; I'd walked right into her playful trap. Now

I'd followed her, she thought I wanted to play – which, of course, I absolutely **DID NOT**.

She sprang out from her hiding place and started barking, if you can call it that; it was actually more of a cute, squeaky **RUFF RUFF** sound. I couldn't help but laugh.

A stretch and a yawn later . . .

It seemed that the puppy would not stop barking, so I turned to go back inside. After all, if she was **HERE**, that meant my favourite snoozing spot was free – but I'd have to be quick or she might follow me.

18

That was my second mistake. Running away from a puppy is a BAD idea (seriously, don't try it) because all that happens is… they chase you even more.

'Yay! Pwaying!' Puppy said excitedly. 'I catch woo!' she said, running after me on tiny paws. Puppy was VERY quick for something so small, and I didn't make it very far.

'Got woo!' said Puppy, pinning me to the ground. 'This is fwun!' she squeaked happily.

'I'm glad to see you're having fun, Cat!' The Lovely Witch said from the doorway again. 'I hoped Puppy would bring out your playful side.'

This went on and on until Puppy finally said, 'Twired!' Then she sank to the ground, falling straight to sleep. This was my chance to escape, and so I sneaked off quickly back inside.

But for the rest of the day, I couldn't sleep. I had to find a way to make sure The Lovely Witch kept me – and not that annoying puppy. I also had to keep one eye open in case the crazed beast found me again. And by dinner time, I was tired and grumpy.

At dinner time . . .

The Lovely Witch placed our dinner bowls down in front of us. Puppy gulped hers down noisily without even chewing it (it was disgusting). And then she just sat there looking at mine.

'NO. This is MY DINNER!' I said, moving my bowl away from her. 'You've already eaten yours!' But as I tried to enjoy my dinner, the puppy just stared at me.

'Hungwy,' she said, resting a tiny paw on mine.

Snatching my paw away, I tried to pretend she wasn't there at all. I wasn't going to let her ruin dinner time too.

Later, after it was dark . . .

As I settled down for a quick whatever-time-of-day-it-is snooze, Puppy tried to snuggle in next to me. And that was it.

'**NOOO!** You cannot sleep here – this is my space! **GO AWAY!**' I yelled.

This time she did listen and scampered off on her own. Good! Hopefully, she'll leave me alone from now on, I was thinking when...

She started snoring loudly. Yes, just when I thought this puppy couldn't be any **MORE** annoying, I found out that it snores too!

I was far too tired for my usual night-time adventures, so, for the first time ever, I just tried to go to sleep instead. But I found it hard to relax, and not only because of the terrible snoring... It started as a little worry, but the more I thought about it, the bigger it got. I wondered whether the puppy was really here to stay. Was The Lovely Witch going to get rid of me? Where would I even go? Would she find me a new home? Was there a chance I could change her mind?

Then it came to me; I'd just have to make sure we spent **LOTS** more time together so I could remind her how perfect we were together. So perfect we didn't need a silly puppy hanging around.

The Annual Witching Meeting must be coming up soon, I thought. That would be the perfect time to show her that I was the best pet ever.

Chapter 3

Go Fetch

I awoke that morning to find an irritating puppy lying across my head, and possibly the worst news ever – even worse than when The Lovely Witch first told me about the puppy.

'Cat, I'm going away for the weekend – it's my Annual Witching Meeting – I'm sorry you won't be coming with me this time. You need to stay here to look after

the puppy,' The Lovely Witch said.

WHAT? I couldn't believe what she was saying. We ALWAYS went to the Annual Witching Meeting TOGETHER. Puppy had even managed to ruin that! And to make things worse, I was going to have to LOOK AFTER it – on my own.

To show The Lovely Witch that I was

very upset, I turned and dashed out into the garden. I didn't want to hear another word from her. I watched from afar as she said goodbye to Puppy – her broomstick in one hand and a suitcase in the other. Before flying off, she shouted out into the garden, 'Remember, Cat, absolutely **NO** magic while I'm away!'

How had this happened!? I didn't know how to look after a puppy? I couldn't even look after myself very well; I had no idea how I would survive this weekend, especially as I was forbidden from using magic – which ruled out the Puppy Sleeping Spell I was thinking of brewing. But as you already know, I don't give up that easily. I just needed something else, something other than ME, to keep this puppy busy.

At breakfast . . .

Whilst trying to enjoy my mackerel (with the puppy watching my every mouthful again), I hatched a cunning plan. FETCH! A game of fetch would be perfect. Dogs love to fetch, don't they!? It would be great because I wouldn't need to move anywhere. I could just stand or lie in one place, throw something for Puppy and wait for her to bring it back to me. Fetch would kill lots of time. It was a great plan.

But it turned out that the puppy had no idea HOW to fetch. Oh, she loved chasing things alright (especially me), but she was not very good at bringing them back. She needed some lessons. I didn't know anything about puppy training, but since when did not knowing something ever stop me? We'd both have to learn as we went along. How hard could it possibly be?

I decided to start with something simple – SIT.

'Sit,' I said to the puppy. But she just stared back at me. 'Sit,' I said again, then again more firmly, 'SIT.' But the puppy just cocked her head and looked at me like I was nuts.

'Oh, for goodness' sake. SIT!' I said

again, this time sitting down myself to show her what I meant.

'Sit,' she repeated... still standing. She really wasn't getting it.

'Yes, SIT!' I was starting to lose my patience. 'YOU sit... Puppy, SIT... like this,' I said, standing and sitting and standing and sitting again.

Ages later . . .

We tried this for a while, but she really wasn't learning. And after all this training, I was starting to feel hungry again. 'Let's have a break and a snack,' I said, reaching for my favourite cat treats.

At the promise of a treat, Puppy started to go bonkers again! 'Hungwy, hungwy!' she kept saying over and over.

'Okay, **OKAY!** Will you just sit down for a—' I started to say, and as if by magic, the puppy SAT down. She gobbled down the treat in an instant then started leaping around again.

'SIT!' I said, more boldly this time, and again she sat down. We had finally mastered it! Treats were the answer... and I could definitely now consider myself an excellent puppy trainer!

Now we had sit sorted, I thought we should go back to my original plan of learning to FETCH. But this time fetch WITH treats! Haha. It was another excellent idea.

With a treat in one paw, I grabbed the ball and threw it as hard as I could across the room. Wow, I didn't realise I could throw that far. I watched, mouth open wide, as the ball bounced off the wall... onto the bookshelf, knocking over a large spellbook. I could barely bring myself to watch as it fell onto another book...

and then another until they were all toppling into each other like dominoes. I held my breath as the last book, The Giant Book of Spells, wobbled before falling and smashing down onto a shelf of potions below. The potion shelf collapsed, sending bottles crashing into the big cauldron underneath.

Puppy didn't seem at all bothered by this – it was like she hadn't even noticed; she was still heading for the ball.

'Bawl bawl!' she cried over and over again. I guess she really wanted a treat because she carried on running – straight towards the disaster that was unfolding before my eyes.

Meanwhile . . .

The potions had been busy mixing together in the cauldron and had started to sparkle and fizz. A kind of glittering rainbow smoke poured thickly over the sides of the cauldron. It began to cover the floor and was heading directly towards the puppy. This was not good at all! I had no idea what this potion might do, and I couldn't let anything bad happen to the puppy... The Lovely Witch would be so disappointed. She'd definitely choose the puppy over me, and I'd be looking for a new home!

So, I dived towards her, trying to knock her out of the path of the potion cloud. But I was too late; instead, we ended up in a big heap with the colourful cloud covering us both.

Chapter 4

The Rainbow Potion

I awoke the following day to the strangest feeling. I knew that something wasn't quite right, but I couldn't put a paw on what it was. As I looked around, I saw the room was in a terrible mess. But I couldn't remember how or why it had happened.

My next thought was, **OH NOOO! I'M GOING TO BE IN SOOO MUCH TROUBLE!**

The Lovely Witch will be so disappointed in me for making a mess! I'd better start packing my bags.

But where on Earth was Puppy? I couldn't see her anywhere, and there was **NO WAY** I was going to tidy all that up on my own. She would have to help me.

'Puppy!' I shouted, my voice sounding weirdly squeaky. That was odd. 'Puppy, where are you?' I squeaked again. This whole time I had been resisting the urge to jump up and down. Strange. I'd **NEVER** wanted to do that before.

Then I heard snoring coming from the windowsill. It must be that puppy, I thought. Snoozing away, expecting ME to tidy up on my own.

Suddenly, I just couldn't stop myself. I got all excited and started... BARKING!

RUFF RUFF RUFF!

It was quite an annoying noise, and worst of all, once I'd started, I couldn't stop. The more I barked, the more excited I got, and this made me want to bark even more.

RUFF RUFF RUFF!

It didn't sound like ME at all, but it did sound like... Puppy! And that's

when I saw **MYSELF**. There I was, asleep
on the windowsill.

Everything came flooding back:

throwing the ball, the books falling, the potions smashing, the cauldron mixing, the glittery rainbow potion cloud swallowing us both up. I realised with horror what must have happened...

'We've accidentally made a switching potion! We've been **SWITCHED**! Now I am Puppy and you are Cat!'

Puppy jumped down from the windowsill gracefully, like a cat. Then she just stared at me as I tried to explain what must have happened – whilst I carried on jumping around.

Oh, I already missed being a cat.

'I a cat... woo a puppy?' Puppy said, confused.

What seemed like hours later . . .

It took me AGES to explain to her what had happened.

'So, we accidentally made a switching potion, and I am ME in YOUR body... and you are YOU in MY body,' I said again.

'I ME... woo... woo?' Puppy repeated, with a puzzled look on her (my) face. This went on for a while. In the end, I wasn't sure who was who, what was what, and what on Earth we were going to do about it.

I'm usually pretty good in the face of a catastrophe, but my mind was muddled. The floppy puppy ears were very distracting too. And instead of trying to find a solution to our problem, I just wanted to chase my own tail. It was ridiculous.

At that moment, Puppy, usually a dog of few words, said the first helpful thing I'd ever heard her say…

'Make new pwotion and fwix it.'

Annoyingly, she was right.

We turned to the spellbooks to find an answer. But, as we flicked through the pages of the books, we discovered that they were all totally ruined. They must have been affected by the potion too; all the words had been switched around and the pages were a total jumble. None of it made any sense. They were useless.

I panicked. We'll be stuck like this forever... or at least until The Lovely Witch comes home... and then I'll get the blame because I was in charge and she definitely won't keep me! I'll be kicked out, and Puppy will replace me!

I gave in and started chasing my own tail.

'Need more bwooks,' Puppy suggested, as I unhelpfully whizzed

around and around in a circle. Puppy was right; we needed some more spellbooks, but where would we find them?

Then it came to me…

'We need to go to The Enchanted Library. The Lovely Witch always goes there and comes home with **LOADS** of books. The place must be full of them!' I squeaked dizzily.

'Libwey!' Puppy agreed.

But where was the library? I'd never been there before. Without a map or a magical direction spell, I was just going to have to go and look for it myself. Luckily,

I seemed to have a new super-sense of smell, which I was sure would be useful. Perhaps I'd be able to sniff out the libwey... I mean library.

A little while later . . .

Leaving the magical mayhem behind, we set off in search of The Enchanted Library – me scurrying along on tiny little puppy paws whilst Puppy slinked along effortlessly. Oh, how I wished to be a cat again.

I wasn't used to going to new places without The Lovely Witch, so I couldn't help feeling a little bit glad that Puppy and I were in this together.

Chapter 5

Into The Woods

I had the scent of books on my nose, and I was sure we were going in the direction of the library. We headed away from the cottage, deeper into the woods and towards the town on the other side. We were already further than I'd ever travelled

on my own (well, apart from that time I went around the world on a broomstick). We cats like being out and about on night-time adventures, but ideally not too far from home.

I was very worried about our switch-around potion problem, but I also couldn't hide my excitement; I was going on an adventure! I was going to fix this mess. I was going to be **UNSTOPPABLE!**

Not long after that . . .

A little yawn escaped me. I realised that after all the morning's excitement, I was feeling pretty tired. Yes, it seemed that puppies do need lots and lots of sleep.

How annoying.

I looked across at Puppy and noticed that she was yawning too.

I decided I would usually be settling down for a whatever-time-of-day-it-is snooze myself by now.

We were deep in the woods, and as the sun broke through the trees above, little sunny snooze-spots appeared on the ground all around us – they were too good to resist.

Puppy said it first. 'I'm twired!' she moaned, slowing to a standstill. Not wanting to waste any time, I tried to keep going. But it was no good; I was so tired that my legs felt too heavy to move. I turned to see Puppy already asleep, snoring loudly. I decided a teeny little doze wouldn't hurt, so I curled up and fell asleep almost straight away.

Later . . .

I awoke feeling refreshed and ready to carry on the journey. But I suddenly had the feeling I was being watched. My first thought was that it was Puppy, but no, she was still fast asleep, so it wasn't her. I started feeling quite nervous. I looked around. I took in the smells and the sounds.

I noticed the chirping of the birds, the creaking and rustling of the tall trees and the earthy smell of mud. I knew something was amiss, but I couldn't tell what.

I realised I had rushed right into this 'plan' as usual – without a thought for the risk. *When will I learn!? There could be dangers I don't know about. There could be monsters... or ogres... or even DRAGONS that live here. And here we are, a little puppy and a cat all on our own.*

That's when I saw the two big, bright, orange eyes glaring down at us from a tree branch above.

Annoyingly, my first instinct was to bark and start jumping about. **'GRRR RUFF RUFF RUFF!'** I said, unsure how that would help anything. It did wake Puppy, though, who jumped to her (my) paws, ready to pounce like a cat.

Seemingly not bothered by my barking or Puppy's fearsome cat pose, the creature with the orange eyes flew down from the tree, landing next to me on the ground.

'Hello there. What are a cat and a

puppy doing here all on their own? Are you two lost?' he asked curiously.

'Oh, haha, it's just an OWL,' I said in my squeaky puppy voice – relieved it wasn't a dragon.

'Um. Excuse me! Don't you know it's very rude to talk about someone whilst they're standing right in front of you!'

'Oh, sorry, it was just that I thought you might be a dragon or an ogre or something scary. I'm very pleased you're an owl. I'm Cat and this is Puppy,' I said.

'Very pleased to meet you. I am Orion the Owl. Let me get this right, **YOU are CAT, and YOU are PUPPY.**' He looked utterly bewildered.

'Yes, it's a long story, but there was this ball, some books, potions, a cauldron and a rainbow potion cloud. Somehow we managed to magically switch bodies, so I'm really Cat, and she is really Puppy. I'm off to The Enchanted Library to find a spellbook, so I can switch us back,' I said in one long breath.

'Fear not!' said Orion. 'I know someone who can help you with your problem, and I can take you straight to him if you'd like?'

'Oh wow, that would be brilliant! Thank you!' I said, jumping about wildly. This was the first bit of luck I'd had, and I was so pleased that Orion had come along when he had.

We followed Orion as he led us on a twisty trail through a deep, dark area of the wood. The trees were so close together that there were almost no sunny snooze-spots anywhere on the ground.

A little while later . . .

As we walked along, I noticed a poster stuck to a tree, it read 'MISSING – Have you seen this cat? Last seen in the woods!' along with a picture of a missing black moggy. Then, a bit further on, I noticed another one saying 'MISSING! Help! Have you seen our darling Doggykins? Last seen on the edge of the woods!' By the fourth poster, I couldn't help feeling a bit worried. I wondered why we were following a complete stranger into the deep, dark woods. We didn't know Orion at all. And who was he taking us to? I'd been very silly not to ask.

'Um. Where was it you said we were going?' I asked, trying to hide the fear from my squeaky puppy voice.

'Oh, don't worry,' Orion said smoothly. 'You'll soon see.'

That answer did nothing to calm my nerves. Looking over at Puppy, she didn't seem to be worried one bit – she obviously hadn't noticed the posters. Silly dog. It would be down to me alone to figure this out.

Just as I thought about making a run for it, we arrived at a crooked little cottage.

'We're here!' Orion announced.

Chapter 6

The Crooked Cottage

I was still thinking of running away, when the door of the crooked cottage swung open and out stepped... a very smart, very kind-looking wizard. He was dressed almost just as you'd expect – with a long, dark blue cloak and a tall, pointy hat... and some novelty cat slippers. Weird.

'Good evening!' he said, smiling at us

warmly. 'I am The Wizard of the Woods, or some people just call me, The Wizard. Orion, are you going to introduce me to your new friends?'

Landing on The Wizard's shoulder, Orion introduced us and explained our switching potion problem.

'I will certainly be able to help you!' The Wizard assured us. 'But, please, it's getting dark now, and you must be very hungry after your journey. Cat and Puppy, or is it Puppy and Cat? Haha! You must come in for a rest and a bite to eat,' he said, laughing, even though nothing he'd said was very funny.

The Wizard seemed friendly and

harmless enough, but for some reason something didn't seem right. I was about to thank him for his kind invitation and make a quick run for it, but when I turned to tell Puppy the plan, she was already heading through the door. I nervously followed her into the cottage. The door slammed shut behind me – all on its own.

The Wizard led us through to his magical workshop. I looked around in wonder. It was amazing; there were shelves upon shelves FULL of spellbooks and potion bottles in every colour imaginable.

There was a big, shiny cauldron in the middle of the room, bubbling away and magically stirring itself. With all this magic at his fingertips, surely The Wizard would be able to help us switch back to ourselves. I felt that our troubles were almost over, so I relaxed – just a little.

'You see! I'm sure I'll be able to help you with your potion problem!' The Wizard said, as though he'd just read my mind. 'But first, let's eat!' And he ushered us into the kitchen.

At dinner time . . .

We all sat together and ate a delicious dinner (that magically appeared before us in a flash of light), whilst The Wizard of the Woods asked us lots of questions. He wanted to know everything about us: who we were, where we lived and everything about The Lovely Witch. By the time we had finished eating (I say WE, Puppy had swallowed hers down in almost one mouthful as usual), we were both exhausted. It had been a **VERY** long day.

The Wizard explained that it was just the two of them – Orion and himself living at the crooked cottage. 'So, it's always nice to have company,' he added before insisting that we stayed for the night. He showed us to the guest bedroom, where we collapsed happily onto a big, fluffy bed and fell asleep almost immediately.

Later that night . . .

I awoke with a start when I heard a strange noise. It took me a moment to remember where I was. I wasn't sure how long I'd been asleep, but when I looked out of the window it was still dark outside.

I heard it again. It sounded like a loud meow. It's okay, it's just a cat, I thought. But wait! The Wizard never mentioned having a cat. Then I heard another noise; this time it sounded like a howl. Could it be a... dog? But again, The Wizard never mentioned having a dog, and I was sure he'd said that it was just him and Orion living together. I began to feel a little afraid.

I went across to Puppy and nudged her awake.

'Twired,' she said with a cat-like yawn.

'Come on, something isn't right here,' I said, nudging her harder this time. 'I just heard some strange noises outside. Let's go and investigate!'

Puppy wasn't happy about leaving the nice soft bed, but when she heard the noises she was too frightened to stay on her own.

As we crept quietly through the creaky, old cottage, the niggling feeling returned; I just knew something was amiss with The Wizard and his orange-eyed owl.

We followed the noises to a large, wooden back door – which had a cat flap. Handy! I was about to pop my head out to see what was happening outside, when something stopped me in my tracks.

'LEAVING SO SOON!?' boomed a voice from behind us. We turned to see The Wizard standing there in the dark, Orion perched on his shoulder. Orion's orange eyes were glowing brightly.

I couldn't help feeling like we'd been caught doing something naughty. But I'm used to that, so, thinking fast, I explained that we were just heading out for some fresh air.

'Ah, well, seeing as you're up, let me introduce you to The **GANG**!' The Wizard said with a terrifying chuckle.

'The Gang? Who is The Gang!?' I managed to ask, nervously.

'You'll see!' said Orion with glee as The Wizard swung open the door.

The garden itself looked like paradise. It was lush green with leafy trees and plants, and there were flowers everywhere. The grass looked like the softest, greenest carpet (almost perfect for a whatever-time-of-day-it-is snooze). There was a stream trickling through the middle, with a little waterfall at one end.

But we were not alone in the garden.

Creatures started to emerge from where they must have been hiding. Puppy and I were frozen to the spot in shock. What was going on? I couldn't believe what I was seeing. The garden was FULL of...

... cats and dogs! All sorts of cats and dogs. Big ones, small ones, fluffy ones, spotty ones, striped ones, black, brown and even rainbow ones. But the one thing they all had in common was that they all looked utterly...

...miserable! They were sulking, skulking, sleeping, weeping, howling, yowling, meowing and scowling.

'EVERYONE, this is Cat and Puppy. Cat and Puppy, this is... everyone!'

The Gang barely looked around, and Puppy and I stood there, speechless, our mouths wide open.

Moments later . . .

'Ah! You're probably wondering why they're all here, why I didn't mention them earlier and why you didn't hear them!' The Wizard said, taking the words right out of my mouth.

'Yeeeees!' said Puppy.

'Well, let me explain. I'm sure that it's not what you're thinking. Here I run a sanctuary for lost cats and dogs. I provide a haven where I make sure everyone is well-fed and cared for. In return, they bring me all the joy in the world. We are like one big happy family. But we haven't had any new arrivals for a while, so you can imagine my delight when you two arrived earlier! I thought I'd let you settle into your new home for a while before introducing you to everyone.'

'New home!? Wow. That's very kind,' I said, managing to speak finally. 'But we're not LOST. We know exactly where we came from and where we're going, or at least we DID before Orion brought us here.'

'Nonsense!' said The Wizard. 'You are clearly LOST and very confused... uttering some tale about a switching potion? Ha. It's absurd. No dog or cat could POSSIBLY concoct a very tricky switching potion. It is all made up – a pack of lies! You obviously need MY help, and I must insist that you stay and let me care for you.'

'You can't just go around rescuing animals that don't want to be rescued!' I said, looking at all the sad cats and dogs. 'We don't need rescuing, and I'm not sure The Gang did either. They certainly don't look very pleased about it!'

'Cats and dogs simply do not know what is good for them!' The Wizard replied. 'You'll see! Come and make yourselves at home...'

We'd heard enough, and, for once, Puppy didn't need a nudge – she was already making a run for the gate at top cat speed.

'STOP THEM!' The Wizard shouted from behind. 'They NEED our HELP!'

The Gang watched us sadly as we went to make our escape.

'Puppy, we can't just leave them here! What shall we do!?' I asked, feeling terrible that we were leaving them all behind.

'WUN!' Puppy shouted to The Gang. 'WUN NOW!'

These words seemed to wake the cats and dogs from their miserable trance, and they were quick to follow our lead.

Before The Wizard could put on his novelty slippers, Puppy had climbed easily over the gate – gracefully, like a cat. Being so small, I squeezed through a gap beneath the gate easily. And The Gang followed closely behind, before happily disappearing off into the woods in all directions.

We had escaped The Wizard for now, but as we ran the fastest we'd ever run before, something told me it might not be the last we'd seen of him.

Chapter 7

The Enchanted Library

We walked all through the night, desperate to get as far away from that wizard as we could. Luckily, with my new super-sense of smell, I knew we were heading towards the library.

'Not like wizard,' Puppy said, looking back to check we weren't being followed.

'Me neither,' I said. The Wizard wasn't my only worry. Would we be able to switch ourselves back? Would we ever get home? If we did, would The Lovely Witch send me away? Well, whatever happened, at least Puppy and I were in it together – for now.

At the break of morning . . .

By the time the sun had risen, we'd finally made it through the woods to the edge of town. Everything was eerily quiet. Whilst the townsfolk were stirring from their sleep, we made our way through the silent streets until The Enchanted Library was in sight.

It was the biggest building I'd seen in my life. It looked almost like a castle, with turrets and towers rising high up into the sky. The outside walls had beautiful shapes and patterns in the brickwork. Stone steps led up to a grand, arch-shaped wooden door. Above the door was a large sign that read, 'Open 24/7 – No Animals May Enter'.

After **EVERYTHING** we'd gone through to get there, that sign was a blow. 'Twired and hungwy', Puppy suggested we give up and head home, but, as you know, I'm not one to give up that easily.

'Come on, Puppy, WE CAN DO THIS. Look, I don't see anyone around,' I said, 'let's just walk straight in through the front door – what's the worst that could happen?'

It took our combined strength (and a lucky gust of wind) to push the gigantic door open enough for us to squeeze inside. But as the door swung shut behind us, we found ourselves face to face with a very stern-looking librarian.

'How did you two get in here?!' she said, escorting us straight back outside. 'We have a strict **NO ANIMALS** policy here, I'm afraid. Don't bother trying again – I'll be watching. If I were you, I'd give up and go **HOME!'** She finished by slamming the door shut behind her.

'That was a bit mean!' I huffed. 'Come on, Puppy, if we can't go through that door, we'll have to find another way in.'

Walking around the outside of the building, we found lots of other ways in, but The Stern Librarian seemed to be everywhere! Every time we tried, we ended up being rudely kicked out again.

After about 25 failed attempts to get inside the library . . .

I was ready to give up, but Puppy surprised me with a BRILLIANT idea.

'I climb, woo jump!' she said, looking excitedly at the wall. Using her super cat-skills, she began to effortlessly scale the wall. It was brilliant! I stood watching in awe as she climbed all the way to the ledge of an upstairs window.

But how on EARTH was I going to get

up there? Did she say jump? It was a long way to jump for a small puppy like me… I stopped mid-thought.

As I looked up at the wall, I noticed pretty patterns in the brickwork. Some of the bricks were sticking out further than others… and would work perfectly well as small ledges for my tiny paws! Now I knew what Puppy meant when she'd told me to jump.

I charged towards the wall, jumping up to the first little ledge, then the next, and the next, and so on until I finally made it to the window ledge where Puppy was waiting.

We found the window was open a

little, and we wasted no time squeezing through the gap. Ha! We'd finally made it INSIDE the library... so far undetected by The Stern Librarian.

The place smelled wondrous... like books, I guess! I looked around at the floor-to-ceiling shelves upon shelves upon shelves of books. There were more books in this place than I could ever have imagined existed in the whole world. It was incredible, but also a bit worrying – where would we even begin to look for the book we needed? It seemed like an impossible task.

But we definitely wouldn't find the right book if we didn't start looking. So, we jumped down from our ledge and crept around quietly until we spotted the Brews, Potions, Tonics & Tinctures section. We began exploring the almost never-ending aisles of books.

A while later . . .

As we worked our way along one aisle, we were startled by two voices that seemed to be coming our way. The voices got louder and louder as they approached. We dived behind a bookshelf so they couldn't see us.

'Yes, I'm looking for a book about

switching potions,' said the first voice.

Through the gaps between the books, we could see that they were only two aisles away from us. There was something familiar about the voice. I was just trying to remember where I'd heard it before when the voice of The Stern Librarian replied.

'Ah, I know just the book! It's right this way!' she said. 'The book you're looking for is called Changing Potions, by S. W. Itch. It's in aisle 217, row 37, under the letter I.'

They started walking towards where we were hiding. We needed to stay out of sight.

'Wizard!' Puppy whispered.

'Yes! You're right, Puppy,' I whispered back, 'it's The Wizard of the Woods! Wait, why is HE looking for a book on switching potions!? I know! He knew WE'D be coming here. He's trying to get to the book before us, then he thinks we'll have no choice but to go back to his sanctuary and live with him forever!'

We sank back down against the bookcase, and as I looked up, I noticed we were sitting beneath the letter I.

'It's here!' I whispered. 'It's somewhere around here. Quick, Puppy, we have to find it before them!'

We scanned the shelves frantically, then there it was... the very book we needed: Changing Potions, by S. W. Itch. I couldn't believe our luck.

Puppy pulled the huge book down from the shelf, and I helped drag it behind the bookcase – out of sight of the fast-approaching librarian and wizard. We hid in silence.

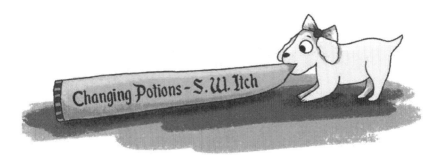

Changing Potions - S. W. Itch

Moments later . . .

'Well, it should... be... here!' came The Stern Librarian's voice. 'Hmm. It's not here, though. Someone must have borrowed it, sorry!'

'Oh, that's a shame! I'll have to come back another time,' replied The Wizard. 'I don't suppose you've seen a ginger cat and a small puppy around here, have you? I've lost my dear pets and I'm desperate to find them!'

'Funnily enough, I **HAVE!**' said The Stern Librarian. 'They've been trying to get in here all morning for some reason, but I sent them on their way, I'm afraid! I suppose you might find them somewhere outside, but there's **NO WAY** they will be in here – we're very strict about our **NO ANIMALS** rule.'

'Ah, okay, thanks anyway,' said The Wizard, as the two of them strode off down the aisle.

Relieved we hadn't been seen, I wasted no time flicking through the pages of the book until I found exactly what we needed.

Switch It Back Brew

'This is it!' I said, then I read aloud the recipe:

- 5 drops of puppy drool.

- 4 whiskers of louse.

- 3 tears of snail (laughing tears, not sad ones).

- 2 teaspoons of ground dragon toenails.
- 1 pinch of magic witching dust.

Directions: Throw it all in, stir and leave for 10 minutes.

'Ha! We've got it, Puppy! This is EXACTLY what we need!'

Chapter 8

Remember, Remember, Remember

Our next problem was remembering the recipe word for word. The book was far too big to take with us, and we didn't have a pen and paper to copy it down. We couldn't rip out the page, that would be wrong; it was one thing sneaking into the library, but quite another to damage a book! No, there was only one thing for it – we needed to remember it.

I looked at Puppy, who was busy grooming herself without a care in the world, whilst I still fought the dog-like urge to chase my own tail. I missed being a cat more than ever.

Puppy and I spent a while repeating the recipe over and over until we couldn't possibly read it anymore. I realised we hadn't eaten since... I couldn't even remember when. Puppy must have had the same thought because she suddenly said she was 'hungwy'.

After a few seconds . . .

I decided we'd looked at the recipe for long enough. 'If we can't remember it now, we never will. Come on, Puppy, let's go,' I said.

I knew if we hurried, we could be out of there, back through the woods, home and switched back to normal in no time. Then we could have a quick tidy round, before eating some nice tuna and then sleep – and all before The Lovely Witch came home.

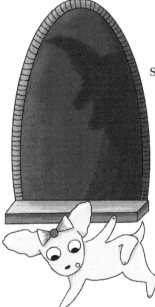

So, with the recipe stored in our heads and something like a plan, we headed back to the window. Unfortunately, getting down from the window ledge was **NOT** as easy as it was to get up.

Puppies, unlike cats, **DO NOT** land on their feet! I have the bump on my fluffy bottom to prove it.

The town was busy with magical folk – witches, wizards, warlocks, pixies and fairies. But they were too busy to notice a cat and a puppy walking together while repeating potion ingredients over and over as they went.

- 6 drops of puppy drool.
- 4 whiskers of mouse.
- 3 sad snails.
- 2 teaspoons of ground dragonfly toenails.

- 1 handful of magic witching dust.

Directions: Throw it all in, stir and leave for 100 minutes...

Not long after that . . .

We made it to the edge of the woods – with the correct potion recipe remembered absolutely word for word. We knew it so well by now I doubted we'd EVER forget it. But just in case, we kept going...

- 5 drops of guppy drool.
- 4 whiskers of grouse.
- 3 sad toenails.
- 2 teaspoons of ground dragon toe scales.
- 1 scoop of magic witching dust.

Directions: Throw it all in, stir and leave for 1 minute.

We were just about to repeat it again when we heard a familiar voice...

'AH HA! There you are!'

I looked up to see Orion the Owl peering down at us from a tree branch. 'Wait here, you two, I'm going to get The Wizard of the Woods. He'll be so pleased I found you! Don't worry, you'll be safe from now on – The Wizard will take good care of you both, **FOREVER!**'

With trying to remember the recipe, we'd totally forgotten all about The Wizard and his owl. Puppy and I looked at each other, and as I looked at my own face, I knew that she was thinking exactly the same thing as me... **RUN!**

And that is exactly what we did.

'Wait! Come back!' we heard Orion shouting from behind. 'You're not safe out there all on your own! You **NEED** us!'

'We don't need you!' I shouted back. 'We already have a home **AND** each other!' (Wow, I never thought I'd hear myself say that. But it was true, we were like...

family.) 'AND The Lovely Witch loves us –
SO GO AWAY AND LEAVE US ALONE!'

I couldn't run and shout anymore, so we ignored the owl who followed behind us, and just ran. We only stopped running when we got home and the front door was bolted shut behind us.

'Home!' Puppy said happily.

'Yes, Puppy, we're home,' I said, realising that it wasn't so bad having a puppy around after all... so long as I wasn't the puppy!

But there was no time to delay – The Lovely Witch could be home at any moment (I actually had no idea exactly when, because I'm not very good at keeping time – but I kind of knew it must be soon).

'Right, Puppy, it's potion time. Come on, let's get everything we need. What did we need again? Wait, was it... oh **NOOOO** I can't remember! **THINK, THINK, THINK!** Wait, I've got it! It was...

- 5 splodges of puppy drool.
- 4 whiskery louse.
- 3 sad tears of slug.
- 2 teaspoons of ground dragon scales.
- 1 sprinkle of magic witching dust.'

'And what were the directions? Ah, yes! Throw it all in, stir and leave... for how long? I can't remember, can you?'

'20 mwinutes,' said Puppy helpfully.

'Yes, that sounds about right,' I said as I started collecting ingredients from the mess that still covered the floor.

A little while later . . .

We had EVERYTHING we needed. Except for the whiskery louse – they all ran away when we tried to catch them, so

we had to make do with a jar of whisker lice. Also, I could only find happy slugs, so their happy tears would have to do. It's harder than you might think to find a sad slug – they're always in such great moods.

It was time to mix the potion and switch ourselves back to normal. What could possibly go wrong!?

Chapter 9

Potion Commotion

Puppy and I threw everything into the cauldron, along with an EXTRA smidgen of magic witching dust for good measure.

'Now we wait for… how long again?!' I wondered aloud.

'Hmmm. One minute!' Puppy replied.

After the longest minute ever…

Nothing happened. The mixture was bubbling away nicely, but it didn't seem to be doing anything.

The first, accidental, potion was wonderfully glittery and rainbow-coloured, but this potion just looked like brown squelchy mud (or something else,

I'd rather not say), and it smelled terrible too, like rotten cabbages and stinky old socks.

'We must have done something wrong,' I said, 'but I can't think WHAT it could possibly be – we followed the recipe to the very letter… I'm sure we did, didn't we!?'

'More, more, **MORE!**' said Puppy, picking up random ingredients and tossing them into the cauldron.

'**NO! STOP!**' I yelled, knowing only too well what happens when you don't follow instructions, but it was too late; Puppy had already added: a **FULL** jar of magic witching dust; an old boot; some silvery

cobwebs; a red-and-white toadstool; a
dusty old witch's hat; some stinky; gone-
off mackerel and loads of other things that
were **NOT** in the recipe.

But as Puppy carried on adding
more things, the potion started to get
going. It turned from the brown sludge
to a beautiful, swirling, dark blue, then it
began to turn bright blue, then turquoise,
mint green, sunshine yellow, orange, red,

pink, purple… it kept going through every colour imaginable. Then, it started to FIZZ AND POP.

I wasn't sure if Puppy was a potion-mixing genius or just CRAZY, but something was happening. I hoped that it was the switching-back potion we had planned and not some other catastrophe.

But just then, we were interrupted by loud banging at the front door, followed by the rattling of the handle.

'Oh no! We're too late! It must be The Lovely Witch home from her meeting!' I said sadly, looking around at the terrible mess everywhere, knowing I'd soon be getting kicked out. There was no way we were going to get away with this. We were going to be in so much TROUBLE.

Despite my panic, I did the most unhelpful thing possible... I started barking (again)!

GRRR RUFF RUFF RUFF!

It was something about the knocking on the door – I just couldn't help myself. But how annoying, now she KNEW we were at home! There would be no hiding from this.

Then came a voice we'd hoped NEVER to hear again: 'I can hear you in there! Come out, little puppy and little kitty cat! There's nothing to be afraid of. It's just ME, The Wizard of the Woods. I've come to rescue you, poor abandoned, confused

little things! Come and open the door.
Don't be scared.'

'Oh no! Orion must have followed us
home and then shown The Wizard where
we live!' I whispered to Puppy. 'If he gets
inside, he'll take us both! Neither of us

will ever see The Lovely Witch again, and we'll be stuck like this forever – you a cat and me a dog! What are we going to do!?'

'Working!' Puppy said excitedly, looking at the cauldron. She was right; something WAS working. Whilst we'd been distracted by The Wizard at the door, the potion had turned a silver colour. A shimmering potion cloud started spewing over the edges of the cauldron. It covered the ground, then began to twist and swirl around into a big circle... creating a sort of twinkly hole in the ground.

We peered into the twinkly hole and were amazed to see ourselves looking back at us... but not like a mirror – it was more like a photograph. It was a picture of us right back at the beginning – just at the moment that Puppy had arrived in the cardboard box. Wow, I really looked miserable and not very welcoming. I thought how selfish and unkind I had been. I'd only been worrying about myself and not how Puppy might be feeling.

Then the picture changed to a new one. This time it was a picture of The Lovely Witch leaving for her meeting, with me running off into the garden. The pictures kept changing right before our eyes, and I understood that they were showing us **OUR** story.

Puppy and I were so busy staring

into the hole, we momentarily forgot what was going on. But then there was a loud **BANG! CRASH!** The front door burst open. In sprung The Wizard and his owl.

'Do not be afraid,' said The Wizard, 'stay **EXACTLY** where you are. I'm here to rescue you, my dears!' Armed with his wand, The Wizard started to cast some kind of spell. It was probably a sleeping spell or something, but we didn't wait around to find out. We both knew there was only one way out of this – and so we closed our eyes and jumped straight into the twinkly hole.

Chapter 10

A Journey Back Through Time

Bright lights flashed by as we fell on and on through the hole. Just when I thought our fall would never end, we landed on a giant, twisty slide.

'Weeeee!' said Puppy, as we slid further and further down the biggest and, possibly, funnest, slide ever. As I looked around, I could see that the bright, flashing lights were not actually lights at all, but more pictures of us – like the ones we'd seen earlier.

There was a picture of us mixing the changing potion. Then one of us running through the woods on our way home. Next we saw a picture of us leaving the library. The pictures kept coming, and I knew what was happening...

'Puppy! I think we are travelling back through time... on a slide! You must have made some kind of time-travelling slide potion! Genius!'

'Beginning,' Puppy replied happily.

'Yes, hopefully we can go right back to the **BEGINNING**, to the moment before I threw that ball for you to fetch – which accidentally started this whole thing. But I've travelled back in time once before, and it's not as easy as you think. We need to make sure we go back to the right time and not some other random time.'

I knew that if we weren't careful, we could end up at any time in history, and I did **NOT** want that to happen. I'd once travelled back to the time of the dinosaurs, and one visit was quite enough.

'Puppy, we have to **THINK** very hard now. It's **VERY** important that we only think about that exact moment – right before I threw the ball for you to fetch. Can you do that?'

'Bawl,' said Puppy, eagerly nodding

her head as we continued to ride down the big slide.

'If I'm right, this slide will take us back to the time we're **BOTH** thinking about – if either of us is thinking about something else, goodness knows when or where we'll end up.'

I worried that it might not stop at all. I didn't know for sure what kind of a potion slide this was... it might keep going on and on forever. And even if it did take us back to the right time, I wondered if I would still be going to a new home. I would miss The Lovely Witch and Puppy terribly. But it was no good worrying now – I needed to do what I had told Puppy to do – **THINK** about that exact moment and hope that it worked.

After what felt like ages...

We were **STILL** sliding down the slide, and the pictures kept coming. By now, the pictures were showing us in The Enchanted Library; we were hiding behind the bookshelf as The Wizard and The Stern Librarian searched for the book.

It took all my might to **ONLY** think about the moment before I threw the ball... and not chasing my tail. Oh, how I wanted to chase my tail. I looked over at Puppy, who was now preening herself, just like a cat.

'STOP, Puppy! You need to think!' I warned.

We were nearing the time where we'd want to get off the slide, and I forced myself to THINK. I thought about the ball, I tried to remember picking it up. I remembered how I hated Puppy back then – how annoying she was. I remembered how terribly mean I had been to her. I tried to remember the moment just before I tossed the ball, and then...

BUMP!

We landed in a heap on the cold tiles of the kitchen floor. We were back, but was it the right time?

I looked around the room and then at

Puppy, who was a **PUPPY!** She was back! I was back! We were no longer each other… we were ourselves, and for the first time in what felt like **FOREVER**, I didn't want to chase my own tail. It was so good to be a **CAT** again!

Puppy, on the other hand, **WAS** chasing her tail.

Everything was tidy too; the books were neatly on their shelves, as were the potion bottles. There was no mess on the floor or any evidence of a magic potion disaster. It was almost as if nothing had happened at all.

Just then, The Lovely Witch rushed into the room.

'Oh, there you are! Cat, I'm going away for the weekend – it's the Annual Witching Meeting. I'm sorry you won't be coming with me this time. You need to stay here and look after the puppy,' The Lovely Witch said as she headed for the front door

– with her broomstick in one hand and a suitcase in the other. But this time, instead of running off into the garden to sulk, like I did the first time, I stayed. And this time, before she left, The Lovely Witch stopped and said exactly what I'd been longing to hear this whole time…

'Oh, Cat, you don't need to feel sad about this. Don't **EVER** forget that we are a **FAMILY** – you and me! But now we have a new member of our family – Puppy. From now on, it will be the three of us together,' she said, scratching our ears. 'I'm going to leave you two behind while I go away so you can spend some quality time together. And I hope by the time I return you will be the best of friends.'

She waved us goodbye before adding: 'And remember, Cat, absolutely **NO** magic while I'm away!'

I was relieved to know that I was staying where I belonged… and so was Puppy. I hadn't liked her at first, but I'd been wrong to judge her before I had gotten to know her properly. As it turns out, The Lovely Witch was right – we just needed some quality time together.

I couldn't believe we'd **TOTALLY** gotten away with the whole switching potion thing. I never get away with anything… well, not when I'm on my own anyway!

Sometime after that...

Puppy and I shared a breakfast of salmon, which I couldn't help but gobble down quickly too (well, I was very hungwy). Then we curled up in our favourite sunny spot for a lovely what-ever-time-of-the-day-it-is snooze.

'I'm sorry I wasn't very kind to you when you arrived,' I said, feeling bad about how I had behaved. 'I was used to it being just The Lovely Witch and me... and I was scared of things changing. But I'm glad you're here now.'

'Mwe too,' said Puppy, snuggling in closer.

'Puppy, I've been thinking, that was

a terrifying but very exciting adventure! Shall we go exploring again soon?'

'Yes!' agreed Puppy. 'With mwagic!' she added.

I liked her thinking. I was actually very impressed with Puppy's potion-making skills – she seemed to know exactly how to mix the perfect potion. And it actually worked too – unlike when I did it on my own. I felt, together, we'd make an excellent team. No, not just a team... best friends.

We fell asleep dreaming of magic potions, exploring the woods, wizards and owls, spellbooks, travelling back through time and, most excitingly, our next magical adventure.

To be continued....

Kirstie Watson

Kirstie is a children's storyteller and indie-author. Her debut picture book, *The Witch's Cat and The Cooking Catastrophe* has sold more than 40,000 copies worldwide.

When she's not scribbling down new stories, she loves to visit schools, where she gets to combine her passion for writing, with a knack for inspiring children to get reading and writing.

Kirstie has two children, Jack and Grace – who both support and inspire her writing.

She's an avid reader and collector of children's picture books. Her favourite thing to do is snuggle up with her little dog, Loxie, with a cup of tea and a good book!

Tilia Rand-Bell

Tilia is an illustrator working on many colourful books all over the world. She has several years experience creating and producing a range of unique and vibrant illustrations for children's books and prints.

Tilia has a huge passion for the environment and equality which comes across in her work.

When she's not drawing, she spends her time daydreaming about new places to travel or finding new places to eat.

She has a cat and a dog – who don't seem to practise magic in their spare time (or maybe that's what they want her to think).

Thank you for buying this book!

I hope you've enjoyed meeting **Cat** and **Puppy**.
Did you know that **reader reviews** are like
MAGIC for an author like me?
They help bring attention to the book, and help
others decide if they'd like to buy it too.
So, if you **like** this book, please consider...

1. Telling your **friends**.

2. **Telling me!** I'd love to hear from you.
Send me a message via:
kirstiewatsonauthor.co.uk

3. Leaving a review on **Amazon** or **Goodreads**.

Kirstie x

Find out more about Kirstie and her books:

www.kirstiewatsonauthor.co.uk

Facebook.com/kirstiewatsonauthor

Instagram.com/kirstie_watson_author